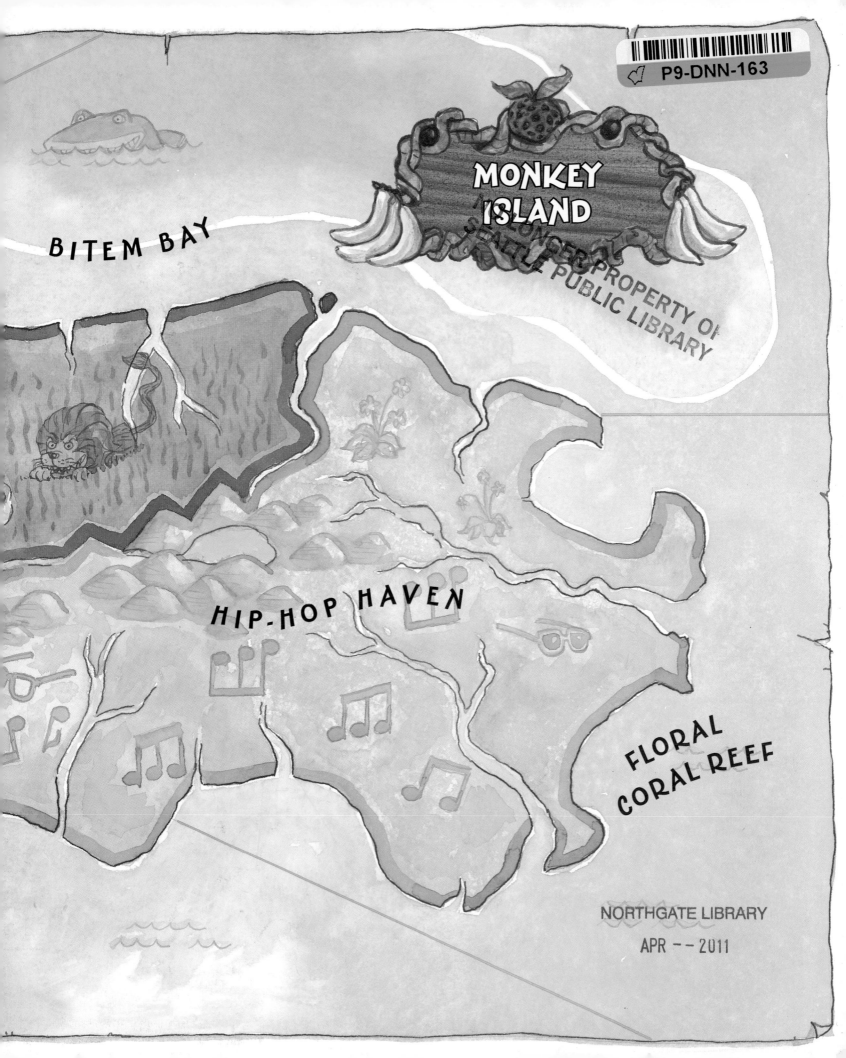

Looking for the Easy Life

Looking for the Easy Life

by **WALTER DEAN MYERS**
illustrated by **LEE HARPER**

HARPER
An Imprint of HarperCollinsPublishers

ife was pretty good on Monkey Island. Yes, it
was. The sun was shining most of the time. The
fruit on the trees was sweet and juicy, and all day long the
monkeys sat around talking their monkey talk and enjoying
their big-time monkey dreams.

"I want every monkey on this island to live good,"
Uh-Huh Freddie said. "And one day this whole island will be
nothing but a monkey paradise." Uh-Huh Freddie was the
Chief Monkey and the hardest-working monkey on the island.
Anything that needed to be done, Uh-Huh Freddie would get
right on it and get it done! Yes, he would.

But then trouble came. Oswego Pete, who was one slick monkey, looked Uh-Huh Freddie in the eye and challenged him for the Chief Monkeydom.

"Good is okay," Oswego Pete said. "But if I become Chief Monkey, I will lead us to the Easy Life, where a monkey don't have to work hard for nothing. All we will have to do is lay back and relax!"

"That sounds good to me," said Drusilla, who was the monkey upon whom Oswego Pete was sweet. "I'm tired of having to stretch all out of shape just to get a banana."

"And none of the monkeys around here are rich enough to bring the Easy Life to us," said Betty Lou. She was Drusilla's best friend, even though she was known to have flirty eyes.

"I think things are just fine," said Beauregard, who was the best-looking monkey on the island. "I don't see nobody walking around here with their belly pinched."

"That is true as far as it goes," Oswego Pete said. "But it don't go far enough and it ain't the Easy Life. I will show you the Easy Life, and then everybody can vote for who they want to be Chief Monkey. Is that fair, Uh-Huh Freddie?"

"Uh-huh," Uh-huh Freddie said, even though he did not like it one little bit.

"Where is the Easy Life around here?" Drusilla asked.

"It's got to be over where the lions live," Oswego Pete said. "I ain't never seen a lion doing no hard work!"

So the monkeys packed up a lunch and traveled over toward where the high grass grew at the foot of a mountain.

They were just about ready to settle down for the night when they heard a loud roar.

"Child, don't let that be no lion," Betty Lou said. "You know how unsociable them things get."

Which was true.

They heard the roar again, and what's more, they smelled some lion stink just before a big-head lion come busting through the brush.

"Hey, Lion, why you making all that noise?" Oswego Pete asked.

"I want something to eat!" the lion roared. "And I think I see some monkey on the menu!"

That lion was as unsociable as Betty Lou said. He started chasing them monkeys faster than the devil could blink his left eye. He was biting and scratching as he ran, while Betty Lou and Drusilla were screaming and screeching. Uh-Huh Freddie and Beauregard were running and jumping. Oswego Pete was halfway up a tree when that lion chomped down on his tail and bit the end of it right off.

It was a pitiful sight. Three of them monkeys was up in the trees and two were hiding in the bushes. The lion sat on a branch below them, chuckling, with the piece of Oswego Pete's tail hanging out his mouth.

"Lion, be a cool cat and throw the end of my tail on up here," Oswego Pete said.

"I had to run after you and catch you," the lion said. "I ain't giving up no tail."

The five monkey friends stayed there, shivering and shaking, until the moon came up and the lion went off to mess with his girlfriend.

Then all five monkeys, one with a piece of his tail gone, slunk off.

"Where we going now?" Drusilla asked. "I'm hungry."

"I sure wish I had me a rich monkey to take me away from all this," Betty Lou said.

"We need to go on home," Uh-Huh Freddie said. "I'm in no mood to be a lion's dinner."

"Amen to that!" Beauregard said, slapping him five.

But Oswego Pete didn't want to hear it.

"We're going down to the seaside," Oswego Pete said. "Fish know how to live the Easy Life. They just swim around all day, float when they want to, and play on the waves. If they get hungry, they just open their fish mouths and eat whatever floats in."

"Sounds good to me," Drusilla said.

"Should have gone there first!" Betty Lou said.

The monkeys went on down to the seaside. Uh-Huh Freddie said he was going to take him a swim. He went into the water, followed by Beauregard, Oswego Pete, and the two lady monkeys. They swam around for a while, and then they hooked their tails together and floated in a big, lazy circle. It was sure nice, and they were all grinning.

But after a while they heard a splashing in the water.

"Child, don't let that be no shark!" Betty Lou called out. "Them things is mean as they want to be!"

They heard the splashing again, and to make things even worse, they started to smell some shark stink.

"Hey, Shark, what you want with your beady-eyed self?" Oswego Pete called. "And how come you ain't got no lips?"

"'Cause I don't want nothing between me and my lunch!" that shark said, with an ugly look on his face.

"Uh-huh!" Uh-Huh Freddie said, and started fast-stroking toward the shore. He got out that water first. The lady monkeys got out the water next, with Beauregard right behind them. Oswego Pete brought up the rear—but he didn't bring it up fast enough, and that shark bit off another part of his tail. He just did manage to get on the shore.

"Mr. Shark, pleeease don't eat no more of my tail," Oswego Pete begged. "Throw it on over here so I can get it."

"Your tail is nothing but a snack, but I worked for it," Shark said. "Come on back into the water and we can talk about it some more."

Oswego Pete knew better than that. He just gave that shark a hard look and flicked a booger at him.

"This Easy Life is going to get us killed!" Betty Lou said.

"And it's not getting us fed!" Drusilla said.

"Uh-Huh Freddie didn't have us running around for our lives," Beauregard said. "Ain't that right, Uh-Huh Freddie?"

"Uh-huh, it sure is," Uh-Huh Freddie said.

"Oswego Pete, if you can't put no food on the table, you got to find yourself somebody else to monkey around with!" Drusilla said.

Now, that hurt Oswego Pete right down to his monkey heart. He knew he had to do something quick. He thought and he thought, and then he figured out what they were doing wrong.

"We need to find someplace where they living the Easy Life and don't eat monkeys," he said.

That's how come Oswego Pete led them over to the river, where some hip-hop hippos lived.

"Yo, Hippos, we are looking to live the Easy Life," Oswego Pete said. "And we see that you are definitely doing just that."

"Hey Up and Hey Lo, that's all good, Bro," one hip-hop hippo said.

"You the funky monkeys we been looking for! We need somebody to hold the umbrellas and keep the sun out our eyes. And you can take all the food you want from the Hip-Hop Hippo restaurant."

"That sounds real easy," Betty Lou said.

"The Hippo Stroll is the way we roll," the hip-hop hippo said. "We rap and we nap, then we nap and we rap, and we do it all with soul."

That's how the monkeys got to be living in the river with the hip-hop hippos. Each one sat on the back of a hippo and held an umbrella to keep the sun out the hippo's eyes. Sometimes they sipped iced tea or just tapped their feet to the rapping hippos' beat.

"This is definitely the Easy Life!" Oswego Pete said.

"I don't know," Beauregard said. "I'm a monkey, not a decoration. I'm getting tired of this."

"And all they eat is weeds and roots and slimy stuff," Drusilla said. "I think they're nasty!"

"Don't get me started," Betty Lou said. "This is so boring, I'm going clean out of my monkey mind."

"I miss my home in the trees," Uh-Huh Freddie said. "I'm going back home."

"But we ain't working hard," Oswego Pete said. "This is the Easy Life!"

"Uh-huh, that it is," said Uh-Huh Freddie. "But it is not the life for no self-respecting monkey. I got some big-time monkey dreams I need to get back to, not hip-hop hippo dreams. I want us all to live good, and I'm ready to do what we need to do to get what I think is due us."

Oswego Pete mumbled something under his breath, but he agreed to go back to San Banana Valley with the others.

With that, the five monkeys packed up their stuff and began the happy trip to their side of the island.

"I think we should keep Uh-Huh Freddie as the Chief Monkey," Beauregard said, giving Uh-Huh Freddie a high five. They had a vote on it by lifting their tails, and Uh-Huh Freddie won by four and a quarter tails.

"It just goes to show you that easy ain't always good," Uh-Huh
Freddie said as they walked along the beach toward their favorite
trees that evening, "and a little work ain't always bad!"

All the monkeys agreed to that. Betty Lou didn't say nothing
much, but she was looking hard over at Beauregard and thinking
maybe she would just settle for a good-looking monkey.

To my sister, Nancy, who
helped me when I fell down
—L.H.

Looking for the Easy Life
Text copyright © 2011 by Walter Dean Myers
Illustrations copyright © 2011 by Lee Harper
Manufactured in China.
All rights reserved. No part of this book may be used or reproduced in any manner whatsoever without written permission
except in the case of brief quotations embodied in critical articles and reviews.
For information address HarperCollins Children's Books,
a division of HarperCollins Publishers, 10 East 53rd Street, New York, NY 10022.
www.harpercollinschildrens.com
Library of Congress Cataloging-in-Publication Data
Myers, Walter Dean, date
    Looking for the easy life / by Walter Dean Myers ; illustrated by Lee Harper. —— 1st ed.
        p.   cm.
    Summary: Five monkeys go in search of the easy life, but find that "easy ain't always good" and "a little work ain't
always bad."
    ISBN 978-0-06-054375-4 (trade bdg.) —— ISBN 978-0-06-054376-1 (lib. bdg.)
    [1. Monkeys——Fiction.   2. Animals——Fiction.]   I. Harper, Lee, date, ill.   II. Title.
PZ7.M992Eas   2010   2008034360
[E]——dc22   CIP
                                                                                                              AC

            11 12 13 14 15   SCP   10 9 8 7 6 5 4 3 2 1   ❖   First Edition